WARREN

# Two Bunnykins out to Tea

Illustrated by

## Glenys Corkery

Viking Kestrel

ALSO BY WARRENER

*A Picnic for Bunnykins*

VIKING KESTREL

Penguin Books Ltd, Harmondsworth, Middlesex, England
Viking Penguin Inc., 40 West 23rd Street, New York, New York 10010, U.S.A.
Penguin Books Australia Ltd, Ringwood, Victoria, Australia
Penguin Books Canada Ltd, 2801 John Street, Markham, Ontario, Canada L3R 1B4
Penguin Books (N.Z.) Ltd, 182-190 Wairau Road, Auckland 10, New Zealand

First published in 1984

Library of Congress catalog card number: 83-23531
British Library Cataloguing in Publication Data
Warrener
Two Bunnykins out to Tea.
I. Title
823'.914[J]    PZ7

ISBN 0-670-80053-8
Printed in Great Britain

The rabbit characters from which the now traditional
Bunnykins ® image evolved were created by an English
nun. Royal Doulton discovered her pencil drawings
in the 1930s and transformed them into the colourful
tableware and figures that have delighted
generations of children ever since.

Royal Doulton's own artists have continued the theme
and today designer Walter Hayward is responsible for
creating new scenes, each telling its own story with
an ageless charm and artistry, for use on their range
of gift pottery cherished by children the world over.

Once upon a bunnytime
two little rabbits said goodbye
to their family for the afternoon.
They were going to tea
with their grandmother.
The little rabbits' names were
Bunting Bunnykins and Babs Bunnykins.
They were brother and sister.

For tea there were lettuce sandwiches,
made from lettuces grown
in their grandmother's own garden.
Grandma Bunnykins knew that
every bunny likes lettuce sandwiches;

but she wished that her two grandchildren
did not grab and gobble quite so fast.

After tea, their grandmother said:
'Before you go home,
I have a present to give you.
It's a dolly that I have made for you.'
She brought it out of her sewing-basket.

The dolly was made of brown cloth
that looked like fur,
and it had a white tail
and long brown ears,
just like a real little rabbit.

Grandma Bunnykins said:
'There! One dollybunny
between two little Bunnykins,
so you'll have to share it.
You'll share it nicely, won't you?'
    'Oh, *yes*, grandma,'
said Bunting and Babs.
    'You'll be sensible little bunnies
and not argue and quarrel and fight?'
    'Oh, *no*, grandma,'
said Babs and Bunting.

They thanked their grandmother,
and Bunting took one cloth paw
of the dollybunny in his paw,
and Babs took the other cloth paw
of the dollybunny in her paw,
and they said goodbye
to their grandmother
and started for home.

No sooner were they outside
their grandmother's front gate
than Babs said to Bunting:
'Dollies are for girls!' And she snatched
the dollybunny from Bunting.

Bunting said:
'Dollies are *not* just for girls.
They're for anyone really small
and young, and I'm smaller and younger
than you are.'

And he snatched the dollybunny back.
'Because I'm older than you are,
I'm stronger!' said Babs.
And she snatched the dollybunny
back again and ran away with it.

Bunting ran after her,
but Babs was older
and stronger and faster:
he couldn't catch up with her.
Then he took off his red jacket,
so that he could run on all fours
like a little wild rabbit.

He ran and he ran

 and he RAN so fast

that he caught up with Babs

and snatched the dollybunny

back from her and ran away with it.

Then Babs ran after Bunting.
At first she couldn't catch up with him;
but then she took off
her little spotted dress,
so that she could run on all fours,
like a wild rabbit.

She ran and she ran

 and she RAN so fast

that she caught up with Bunting

and grabbed at the dollybunny

to snatch it back.

This time Bunting did not let go.
He hung on to the legs of the dollybunny,
and Babs pulled on the arms
and head of the dollybunny.
Bunting bit Babs
with his sharp little teeth
to make her let go; but she wouldn't.

Instead, she scratched Bunting
with her sharp little claws
to make *him* let go; but he wouldn't.

    So there they were:
one pulling on the legs end
of the dollybunny,
and the other pulling on the head end
of the dollybunny.
They pulled and they pulled
and they PULLED.

At last
there was a dreadful tearing sound,
and the poor dollybunny
came apart in the middle.

Bunting sat down suddenly
holding the legs end;
and Babs sat down suddenly
holding the head end.
   Then, 'Oh, dear!'
they both said together.

Very, very sadly
they put on their clothes again and
went back to their grandmother's house
to show her what had happened.

'Well! You were silly bunnies
to quarrel and fight!'
said their grandmother.
'Now you've nothing to play with.'

'Could you sew the two halves
of our dollybunny together again?'
asked Bunting.

'If you did,' said Babs,
'we'd never, never quarrel over it again.
We promise.'

'We promise,' said Bunting.
'On bunny honour.'

'I'll see what I can do,'
said their grandmother.
'Come back tomorrow at tea-time.'

The next day
Babs and Bunting went to tea
with their grandmother again.
They were *very* well-behaved
little bunnies this time.
They said please and thank you
and were careful not to grab and gobble
the lettuce sandwiches.

There was no sign of the dollybunny.

After tea, they asked their grandmother
if she had sewn the two halves
of their dollybunny together again.

Their grandmother shook her head
and said, 'No.'

Then Babs and Bunting
looked very doleful.

Their grandmother said:
'Fetch me my sewing-basket',
and they did.

Then she said:
'I'm going to give back to Babs
the head half of the dollybunny
that I gave you both,
and I shall give back to Bunting
the legs half of that same dollybunny.'

Their grandmother reached
into her basket and took out
the head half of the old dollybunny,
but she had made a new legs half for it,
and sewn the two halves together
into one whole dollybunny
that was for Babs.

And she also took from her basket
the legs half of the old dollybunny,
and she had made a new head half for it,
and sewn the two halves together
into one whole dollybunny for Bunting.

'There!' said their grandmother.
'A dolly for each of you,
instead of a dolly between you.'

'Oh, thank you, thank you!'
the two little Bunnykins cried;
and they hugged their dollybunnies
and danced round and round for joy.

'And when you next come to tea,'
said their grandmother,
'I'll show Bunting
how to make a little jacket for his dolly,
and I'll show Babs
how to make a little dress for hers.
That's a promise.'
   So the two little Bunnykins
went happily home to their family,
each with a dollybunny to play with.
And their father and mother said:
         'Little bunnies always should
          Play together and be good.'
      And that is the end of this bunnytale.